The exploding boy
and other tiny tales

About the author
Nick Parker lives on the outskirts of town. By day he's a creative director of the language consultancy The Writer. By night he writes his tiny tales – at an excruciatingly slow pace. If you want him, he's *spigmite@gmail.com*, or *@nickparker* on twitter.

About these stories
A few of these stories have appeared (occasionally in slightly different forms) in the following places: 'The Exploding Boy' first appeared on *mcsweeneys.com*. 'The Boyle Curriculum' and 'Summer of the Pakflake' were both read on *BBC Radio 4*. 'The Field of Ladders' was first published in *Ambit 156*, and later in *Tales of the Decongested*, Volume One, published by Apis Books. 'Adventure!', 'The Technical Fault' and 'Autobiography of Erik Satie' were all published in *The Enthusiast Almanack*. Faraj Sarkoohi was first published in *PEN International*, Vol 60, No1. Spring/Summer 2010. 'The Museum of the Sea' was first published in *Sea Stories*, an anthology published by the National Maritime Museum. Found report: idea for a photon canon are words found through a google search, and altered.

About the cover
The cover photograph is used by kind permission of Tadeusz Deregowski. You can see more of his paintings, photographs and monoprints at http://tadeuszderegowski.blogspot.com

Thanks to
Tales of the Decongested reading nights for the chance to hear many of these stories come alive; the Royal Festival Hall, for the free seats; Sonali Chapman for her proof-reading eye; Tanya Cornish for her entrails.

The Exploding Boy
and other tiny tales

Nick Parker

spigmitebooks

spigmitebooks

Published by spigmitebooks
37 Thames Avenue, Berkshire RG8 7BY, England
www.nickparker.co.uk

Copyright © Nick Parker, 2011
Cover photograph and inside photograph
copyright © Tadeusz Deregowski, 2010

The moral right of the author has been asserted.
(We had a special 'asserting ceremony' and everything.)

Printed by createspace.com, on the internet

This book is sold subject to the condition that you won't rip it off,
copy bits and pretend you wrote them, try to pass it off as your own,
repackage it, rejacket it, resell it in another form without telling me,
or otherwise dick about with it.

for dad (doi)

Contents

the exploding boy	1
a new type of fire	2
the field of ladders	3
the technical fault	8
the chuckling boxes	9
the joggers	10
the boy with stones for eyes	11
the flood	13
adventure! (for charley boorman)	14
why we cannot defeat the enemy	17
the greatness of the forger	18
the interview	20
the goat tetherer attempts to make history	22
the autobiography of erik satie	23
summer of the pakflake	24
so close	31
the shortage at the petting zoo	32
the minister of defence forgets	33
knots familiar to donald crowhurst	36
the year of weeping	37
the people next door	40
portrait of a life...	41
a clarification	42
the belgian copper crisis	43
the horse killer	45

fragments from the history of pest control	*47*
the boyle curriculum	*51*
why the national anthem turned out rubbish	*58*
the muteness of things	*59*
storage	*64*
found report: idea for a photon canon	*66*
disquiet with the birds	*68*
blink	*69*
snow	*70*
the new buildings	*71*
the dogs	*72*
the stone rains	*73*
the long way home	*75*
cleaning the river	*78*
Faraj Sarkoohi	*79*
the unfrozen	*80*
lightning	*82*
the museum of the sea	*83*

the exploding boy

WE ONLY CALL HIM the Exploding Boy now, of course; retrospectively. For most of last year he was known only as Ticking Boy, which wasn't nearly so dramatic and led mainly to teasing by us, I'm ashamed to say. It would certainly have won him more friends had he been known as Exploding Boy from his first day, instead of his last. You wouldn't steal the lunch money off someone called Exploding Boy. The bigger boys wouldn't have made an Exploding Boy dive for goldfish in the toilets. Being called Exploding Boy could have made him the most popular kid in the playground.

But Ticking Boy? That's asking for it, really. And it wasn't like it was a quiet ticking either. Sometimes, in lessons, you could see that even the teachers were irritated with him, as they raised their voices to be heard.

It would be fair to say that his transformation from Ticking Boy to Exploding Boy was sudden and unexpected. Peter Mathers was certainly caught off-guard, engaged as he was in sticking chewing gum on Ticking Boy's back. It took the caretaker three weeks to clear Peter from the walls of the sports hall, standing on his ladders and reaching with his mop as high as he could to get the last of the bits off.

Talk of Exploding Boy is now chiefly laced with awe and wonder, and estimations of how far away the blast could be heard. Some say as far away as Bloxwich even. We mutter silent prayers of apology for our cruelties, and are lobbying the teachers for a Detonation Day in commemoration.

a new type of fire

WE ARE in need of a new type of fire. We admit that the fires that we already have are all perfectly good fires: the fires for burning logs for warmth; the fires for lighting cigarettes; the fires for burning books with. We have these and many other fires. But we are in need of a new, more efficient type of fire, a fire that will be commensurate with all of today's exacting flammability requirements. A modern fire, if you will.

Just think: more and more these days, people are flinching from fitting smoke alarms. The idea that fire is a risk is so undignified. All those flames, flopping hither and thither in such a random way. Fire has become just too banal for its own good. These days, helicopters fitted with racks of thermal imaging devices buzz the skyline. If they detect a fire in your home, they will send you an email. Fire alarms are so... well. Alarmist. We sympathise, we really do, but there just isn't enough room for all the helicopters.

Fire, we say, is an out-moded kind of a thing. We need a fire for the new digital age. A fire that is streamable, downloadable, scalable, printable, storable in hard drives, retrievable and searchable.

Fire, we say, is badly in need of an upgrade.

* * *

the field of ladders

I

WE WENT to see the field of ladders. I had tired of it after the seventh visit, but Malta hadn't, so there we were again. The ladders are the old-fashioned kind mostly, straight and wooden, with shiny worn rungs from the passing of many feet, starting in the ground, rooted like trees, and going straight up into the sky, where they stop, reaching nothing. Some of the ladders are tall enough to poke at the low-scudding clouds, others barely make it a few feet from the grass. Malta stares in wonder, as she always does, mouthing silently to herself. I watch her lips. Perhaps she is counting the rungs? Once we would have come here together and laughed, given the ladders names, drunk cider in their shade and found beauty in their awkward angles of leaning. Now Malta wanders off alone and the thought of cider makes me queasy and when I try to name a ladder the best I can do is 'Matthew'.

Malta returns from examining a cluster of step-ladders, saying that she thinks she likes the short ones best, they seem contented, and the view from the top doesn't make you dizzy, and they remind her of a friendly uncle she used to visit as a girl. She's wrong of course. The tall ladders are best, and I say so: I say I find their sky-reaching soothing and optimistic, that going as far as they can go is what a ladder should do, and that the short ladders are distasteful to me, with their stumpy and pointless efforts. They are slack ladders, I say. They should put more effort in.

Malta sighs, goes over to a very tall ladder which is moving slowly in the breeze and touches one of its lower rungs. Yes, she says, maybe you're right, the tall ones are rather peaceful. All of a sudden I find my feelings are reversed: I see without doubt that the short ladders are indeed squat and friendly, like they know they could have gone higher but have chosen to take things easy. It's not like there's anything up there to reach, they're quite obviously saying. They are casual and pragmatic ladders. Whereas the tall ladders now seem presumptuous and arrogant, with all their skyward thrusting.

Don't be ridiculous, I snap. Where do they think they're going, huh? Those tall ladders need to get a sense of perspective, I say. I realise that Malta is looking at me. She is mouthing to herself again.

We stand a while in silence, while the shadows of the ladders gradually lengthen in the evening sun. How has it come to this, I think, disagreeing over the height of unreaching ladders? At the same moment, we both notice that in a far corner of the field, a queue of people has gathered. Let's go and look, Malta says, tugging at my sleeve like a child.

We join the line and wait patiently. Malta seems contented. After a long while, we are at the front of the queue, at the foot of the tallest ladder in the field. I watch Malta's lips again. This time I can tell what she is saying: just the right height.

She turns to me. You stay here, she says.

11

WE KNOW what they call us when they think we're not listening. They call us the 'ladder-loons' or the 'rung-nutters', or worse. They forget, of course, that we have with us at all times highly sensitive recording equipment, so sensitive that if we position our microphones correctly, we can hear the fibres in their clothes creak as they breathe. So picking up a half-whispered insult at two hundred yards is no problem to us, even if it is mouthed behind a cupped hand. Latimer says we should ignore these insults. He says people are just jealous of the things that we hear.

Our microphones aren't switched on to monitor cruel words, though. Our microphones have a much nobler purpose. We use them to record the songs of the ladders. When the wind comes in from the east, funnelled by the ridges of the mountains, it blows through the ladders in complex ways, and they give out the most beautiful keening sounds. The tall ladders (which we call 'Hoffnüngs') give out pale and soft notes, notes which induce swooning. Latimer says they are like baby oboes calling for their mothers. The small ladders (which we call 'Cobbetts') have deep, clear tones, which Latimer says is how the moon would sound, if only we could run out a boom long enough to record it. The ways in which the winds eddy and swirl can make several ladders sing together, so that the air folds over and over itself in great swoops of ladder-song. Sometimes we come here intending to set up our equipment, only to find that we can do no more than sob at the beauty of it all, and we have to use the spongy bits off our microphones to wipe away our tears.

Occasionally we argue about which we like best, the sweet sounds of the Hoffnüngs, or the rich tones of the Cobbetts. We can never agree. And what is worse, when we play back our tape recordings, mostly all we get is a sound like static and twigs – just tiny rasps and the clatter of leaves. This is distressing to us because, as Latimer says, if only more people could hear the ladder-song, the world might be a better place, by a rung or two.

Latimer is of the opinion that the ladder-song is the sound of the ladders communicating with each other in a musical tongue. We are of the opinion that perhaps, at times, Latimer can be a bit of a rung-nutter himself. Tonight he has climbed up a Hoffnüng with a cello strapped to his back, and he means to wait for the storm-winds, when he says he too will talk with the ladders and thereby learn their secrets.

We have run out the microphones in readiness. We anticipate quite a performance.

III

THE FIRE-FIGHTERS said afterwards that yes, they had received a call saying there was a woman who looked as though she was about to jump. They said it had been difficult to make out exactly what was said, on account of a terrible racket going on in the background. Those who had heard the call said it sounded like oboes perhaps, although some say they also heard strings.

The fire-fighters said that it was funny, really. They had rushed there in their engines, and had made haste running out their telescopic ladders, only to look around and realise that *their* ladder was somewhat surplus to requirement! You had to laugh, they said.

Although, they added swiftly, no, stopping for a quick laugh in no way compromised their performance as a rescue service, and couldn't possibly have accounted for what happened next.

The fire-fighters say it wasn't like she jumped, exactly. It was more like she just decided to let gravity take its course.

They say yes, it is indeed highly irregular that although she was observed taking to the air, she seemingly did not hit the ground.

The fire-fighters concluded wearily by saying no, whatever the nutter with the cello might have said afterwards, the wild and curious wailings were definitely not emanating from the ladders themselves, and however closely you might listen to those tapes, they in no way suggest that the disorientating crescendos had somehow thickened the very air around her, and buoyed her up, and carried her away on a strange and beautiful lattice of sound.

* * *

the technical fault

DUE TO the technical fault, we had to cancel a number of things yesterday: the parade in your honour; the chat show; the witch hunt.

I spent most of the evening carrying bunting back to my garage and dismantling the floats. I was cross about the fault, naturally, but at least I was occupied.

Those who were forced to come back early from the witch hunt were more vexed: not only did their new wooden torches go unlit, when they got in they found there wasn't even anything to watch on the telly.

* * *

the chuckling boxes

THERE HAS been an accident at the box-packing factory, where your father worked. We understand from the formal statement that he was crushed by many boxes. We are very sorry. This week, they said, the factory has been packing up motion-sensitive laughing greetings cards that give twelve seconds of chortling to accompany your own personal message.

When the forklift truck ran out of control, it seems that they were activated. If it is any consolation, we're sure that the last thing your father heard was the sweet sweet sound of happiness.

* * *

the joggers

THE NEW JOGGING craze makes us nervous. And more and more people are taking it up. All those people heading out for their morning jog as they've done for years, only now they're not putting on their running shoes or their tracksuits or their running shorts. No. They're just heading out in their normal clothes. The sound of their shoes clack-clacking on the pavement, the sight of their jackets, blazers, blouses, shirts, ties, billowing out behind them – it makes us quite nauseous, if we're honest. We look like an entire city's worth of people, all running for buses. Or else a population fleeing from some kind of natural disaster or alien invasion. Only doing so calmly, steadily, at a ten-minute mile pace, and while carrying an isotonic sports drink.

* * *

the boy with stones for eyes

I once knew a boy who had stones for eyes. Oh, he could see with them just fine. But they were heavy. So heavy. He could look down at the ground perfectly well. He was very well acquainted with the sight of his own shoes. But anything above that was troublesome.

If you, a stranger, were to walk past him and were to say hello, he wouldn't answer back. He'd just keep walking, with his head down. You'd probably think he had no manners at all. But it's just because his eyes are too, too heavy to lift.

Over the years, he's worked out ways of dealing with his affliction. If he wants to talk to you for any length of time, he'll lie flat on his back and stare straight up at the ceiling. You'll have to stand over him and look down. Or else he'll rig up a sort of periscope contraption with mirrors, so it's like you're standing facing each other. (The boy with stones for his eyes has such a contraption at home.)

If he needs to look at something quickly, he'll use his special head toss, like a lion tossing his mane. But it takes a lot of effort, needs a few seconds notice, makes his neck hurt and the momentum usually topples him over. Let's just say he's not big on the casual glance. If he shoots you a look, you better know he means it.

We met at the fayre. He was standing by a man selling helium balloons, smiling a too-wide smile.
As I got nearer, I realised he'd got three or four balloons tied to each ear. He caught me staring. I looked away.

'Wait,' he said. 'Let me look at you.'

'What's with the balloons?' I said.

'They help me see,' he said.

'You're making me uncomfortable. Are you going to stare for much longer?'

'Until the balloons go down,' he said.

* * *

the flood

IT HAS been raining for one hundred and thirty-three days straight. Reports are coming in every day of floodings in the east, of valleys filling up, entire villages going underwater. In the west, astonishing footage is being beamed back of a whole mountain that has become unstable because so much of the surrounding earth has been washed away. We haven't seen Mary in a week, not since she stormed out without her life-jacket.

In the meantime, we tune in practically every hour to watch the mountain's slow progress towards collapse, eager for the looped footage of splashdown. Everything seems to be floating away. Day after day stuff rolls past the windows of our house, semi-submerged, tumbling over and over in the floodwaters. We find our thoughts of Mary are no longer watertight.

The mountain still refuses to succumb, though the footage shows it to be practically inverted, now merely a triangle standing on its point, waves breaking all around it. Our thoughts of Mary have become unmoored. We begin to think that the best we can hope for is that something else might float by to take her place.

* * *

adventure!

MAKE WAY! We are the adventurous! And we're going on an adventure!

We're going on an adventure around the world. Not for us the sour milk of mere existence! We sup only on the rich cream of experience! Make way! We're off to test our mettle, to see what we're made of. We're going on an adventurous round-the-world sort-the-men-from-the-boys, the wheat-from-the-chaff, the sheep-from-the-goats adventure.

Who knows what lies ahead? Who can tell how we'll fare? These are not matters that concern us. We're just going to roll up our sleeves, throw caution to the wind, grab life by the horns, feel the wind in our hair and head for the border. Yes, we'll be flying blind, by the seat of our pants, by the skin of our teeth, close to the wind, into the eye of the storm, under the radar, against all odds – and that's how we like it! Give us the raw flesh of vitality over the feeble salad bar of conformity any day. Make way! We're going on an all-terrain, cross-continent, full-throttle whirlwind of reckless free-wheeling adventure!

We've got advisers, obviously. I mean, we're go-getting, frontier-pushing, out-on-a-limb danger whores, not paperwork jockeys! We've got bigger fish to fry, taller mountains to cross, wider streams to forge. If someone offers to secure a few visas, book a few flights, arrange a few transfers, who are we to say no? Did Edmund Hillary knit his own ropes? Did Scott of the Antarctic breed his own huskies? Let others spend their time dabbing their clean-shaven chins with the tepid aftershaves of detail and drudgery – for us it's the great bushy beards of spontaneity! Make way!

Although if we happen to be able to procure a linguist, say, to give us a few pointers on a selection of the local dialects, who are we to say *no, non, nieta, ni, nahna*? We're wheelie-pulling, bear-hugging, life-affirming experience leeches, but we're not going to look mouthwards, gift-horse wise.

Ditto, of course, the medical specialists. It goes without saying that we're rock'n'roll, no-holds-barred, life-less-ordinary-living, continent-straddling thrill-felchers, but we're not lunatics! Twenty-four hour medical assistance isn't the sort of thing you can just turn down! Just think – we're entering the valley of the shadow of the jaws of the unknown once-in-a-lifetime feel-the-fear-and-do-it-anyway adventurous adventure here, you think we want to risk all that being de-railed by having, say, an ingrown toenail go septic? No we do not! We just want to be able to get the thing fixed up and carry on! Who has time for such trifles when adventure is to be had? Not us! Make way!

And if you think the satellite tracking, the driver, a mechanic, two minders and a small team of chefs is in any way incompatible with being a reach-for-the-stars, touching-the-void, high-rolling adrenaline chaser, then my friend you clearly don't know much about adventure! Keep both hands free at all times to grab life round its shapely waist, throw it across your knee and kiss it deeply on the mouth. You think when the chips are down, the stakes are high, the odds are against us, there'll be time for making sandwiches, quibbling over left or right, chatting to locals hassling us for coins or wanting to show us their smelly homes?

Camera crew, corporate sponsorship consultants, financial advisers, stylists, media negotiators, publishing assistants, merchandising licensers, IT trouble-shooters, nutritional schedulers, armed response units, helicopter gunships at all times surveying the terrain from four thousand feet: you're seriously telling me you'd go anywhere at all without these firmly in place? What do you think this is – some kind of game?

* * *

why we cannot defeat the enemy

WE CANNOT defeat the enemy because there is a problem with our highly advanced weaponry. The problem is that our weapons are now so brilliant, so subtle in the prosecution of their goals, that we have found that oftentimes, the enemy does not seem to understand that he is under attack.

We have tried explaining their brilliance and subtlety to him – about how it means we no longer have to blow him to bits and burn his houses and whatnot. But mostly he does not listen. Mostly he just throws rocks at us and smashes up our checkpoints.

We will have to return to using the blunt and brutish weapons, which we hoped we'd all grown out of. This is entirely the fault of the enemy for not being smart enough to know when he has been beaten. So once again it's all clobbering and rending, exploding, pulverising and mashing the enemy. He's only got himself to blame.

This is maddening to us. And if the enemy were smarter, it would be maddening to him too, but right now he is too busy running for his life to give the situation much thought.

* * *

the greatness of the forger

THINGS BEING what they are these days, you can imagine that nobody exactly hangs out a shingle saying *forgeries here while u wait*. But you only have to put your ear to the ground for a few moments to realise that the whispers are insistent and unanimous: Jackson is your man; his forgeries are flawless; his technique is unsurpassed; his equipment is the most modern that money can buy. The rumours say that Jackson had his cameras and scanners smuggled in from America. This in itself, the whispers intimate, is proof enough of the greatness of his powers. But most of all, the whispers say: look around. Do you ever see or hear of anyone who has been stopped at the borders with a Jackson passport? A Jackson forgery is like magic. You will melt away like a ghost in the morning sunlight.

So we have gathered our meagre savings and come to this lop-sided alleyway and knocked on the door just as the whispers have instructed. And a man with a face that is eighty per cent beard and twenty per cent spectacles has clapped us on the shoulder warmly and hustled us inside. We have sat in a back room, snug in the thick embrace of the smell of printing inks and nervous tension.

We have had our pictures taken with cameras that look complex and searching, and seem more related to X-ray machines. We have watched our faces be flipped and magnified on screens. We have watched Jackson's fingers ripple over keyboards, work minutely with paintbrushes, rub delicately at shiny foils and thick papers with watermarks deep within them. And, finally, we have held in our hands those precious blue books that are our tickets to freedom, our talismans which, we hope, will make us, too, melt away at the borders like so many before us.

We are soon back out again in the alleyway, with our ears still tingling with Jackson's whispered instructions as to how to make the passports as old and weathered as we are ourselves.

And so now we stand in line, afraid even to breathe too deeply lest it disturb the fragile atmosphere that surrounds the checkpoint. We finger the corners of our passports, a final weathering. Here, we are beyond even the reassuring hum of the whispers that once spoke of Jackson's greatness.

It is then that we feel a clap on the shoulder, heavy and cold and somehow familiar, and all at once we realise there is another explanation for why nobody with a Jackson forgery is ever seen or heard of again.

* * *

the interview

THE INTERVIEW had been going pretty well, I thought. I had made it clear early on that although I had no specific knowledge of the air filter industry, I was sure that my previous experience with water filter systems – both domestic and industrial – would stand me in good stead. The questions they asked were quite technically demanding, but I felt that I was fielding them well. The parallels between water filtration and air filtration are, after all, pretty numerous.

Just as the panel were relaxing and I had poured myself a second glass of water, they said: 'This is the last question, Mr Lancaster. We'd like you to give us an example of a time when you have used your imagination and ingenuity to solve a difficult problem. You may illustrate your answer with examples from either your professional or your personal life.'

I thought about it for a moment, and then said: 'Every year I send my father exactly the same Father's Day card. I bought it several years ago from a gift shop on the coast. It is quite big, almost the size of an A4 piece of paper. It is printed on thick, glossy card. I suppose you could say that it is quite tacky, really. It's probably made by the same people that make those cheesy Valentine's Day cards that come in boxes, with padded hearts on them. On the front of the card in big, brightly coloured capital letters, it says: DAD! YOU'RE ONE IN A MILLION. Inside it, in biro, I have carefully written the words: No you're not. You're a fucking cunt.

I pop the card through his letterbox on the day before Father's Day. Then, the day after, as soon as my father goes out to work, I break into his house, steal the card back, and store it away for next year. Then I telephone my father, and suggest we meet for a drink. We meet up and chat cordially about this and that. Neither of us has ever mentioned the card.'

'And what problem were you solving with these actions?' asked one of the panel.

I said I would have thought that was obvious.

* * *

the goat tetherer attempts to make history

OUR WHOLE province is ruled by El Primo and his terrible passions. Goat shooting is his current obsession. He has always liked to shoot: birds, tigers, those who displease him. The valley cringes when the blasts ring out. In a way which we cannot express, we have come to despise the goats – the ease with which they die, their seeming acceptance of their lot. The way that they remind us of ourselves.

Every Saturday my job is the same. I bring the herd up from the valley and tether them one by one to posts along the forest trail. I make sure to tie them so that when the hunting party rounds the corner, El Primo is looking the goat straight in the eye. He seems to like it that way. As soon as I hear the shot, I move on ahead, to ready the next one.

But not today. When El Primo reaches the final post, just shy of the crest of the hill, things will be different. As well as the goat, he will find me. And five kilos of dynamite, the fuse already fizzing.

As El Primo rounds the corner, I pray this: in a hundred years' time, in a classroom somewhere in this valley, a teacher will ask: 'Class, who can tell me about El Primo?'

And a child will raise his hand, and snigger, and say: 'Wasn't he the man killed by an exploding goat?'

* * *

the autobiography of erik satie (abbreviated)

[1] I wear white socks and a white vest, along with a velvet coat, soft felt hat and flowing tie (which is partially hidden by my beard), and on my nose I wear my pince-nez, of course.

[2] My expression is very serious. When I laugh, it is unintentional and I always apologise, very politely.

[3] I breathe carefully (a little at a time), and dance very rarely. When walking, I hold my ribs and look steadily behind me.

[4] For a long time I have subscribed to a fashion magazine.

[5] My only nourishment consists of food that is white (I spare you the details for it sounds revolting).

[6] Before writing a work I walk around it several times, accompanied by myself.

[7] My doctor has always told me to smoke (cigarettes, of course). He even explains himself: 'Smoke, my friend. Otherwise someone else will smoke in your place.'

* * *

the summer of the pakflake

WELCOME to www.remembertheflake.com. Click here to enter. We have set up this homepage as a reminder, a tribute even, to those strange few weeks in our history that have come to be known as 'the summer of the pakflake'. Or should we say those strange few weeks in our history which have now been almost completely forgotten as the 'summer of the pakflake'. It seems incredible to us that this time should slip so readily from people's minds, but then that's just the way of things. After all, who now remembers the Millennium Bug? Would the stock-markets get deleted? Would there be global panic, mob rule, rioting, and a general failing of traffic lights? Would it be Abort, Retry or Fail? How quickly we forget how we were all told to stockpile tinned food. How quickly we forget the £79.99 we spent on pointless Windows upgrades.

But we digress. Please browse around the site and re-acquaint yourselves with that strange and unsettling summer, when a seemingly innocuous packaging peanut had us all in such a frenzy.

Click here to continue.

HERE, as they say, is the science bit: a 'packaging peanut' is usually a small polystyrene kernel, roughly the dimensions of a monkey nut. Hence, obviously, the name. Although Pakflakes™ looked like regular polystyrene 'packaging peanuts', they were actually made from a blend of extruded rice starch and gluten. So, unlike traditional polystyrene packaging materials, they were completely organic and dissolved on contact with moisture. Their manufacturers, GreenFlake Industries, were pretty pleased with themselves. They had created an environmentally sound, fully biodegradable packaging material. Had they found the holy grail of packaging materials? And was the holy grail in fact gluten-based? It certainly looked that way. The only downside was that the manufacturing process was more expensive than that of traditional polystyrene peanuts, so GreenFlake were having to charge more for their peanut. And nobody was buying. The market for loose-fill packaging peanuts is extremely price sensitive, as we're sure you can imagine. Not only that, but the Federation of Polystyrene Packaging Manufacturers is one tough cartel. They weren't going to welcome some fancy rice-gluten hybrid onto their patch without a fight. They let it be known sneeringly in the press that consumers wouldn't give a monkeys whether their peanuts were biodegradable or not.

GreenFlake Industries were understandably concerned, and had employed the services of the trendy London advertising agency, Bellinger and Bellinger, to work on 'strengthening their brand image'. They felt that if they could raise awareness of the Pakflake's environmental benefits, consumers might start demanding that their products be packaged using Pakflakes™, thereby creating what Mr Bellinger himself assured them was excellent 'marginal utility leverage'. He showed them some pie-charts which seemed to bear this out. And a Powerpoint presentation.

Our research suggests that on the afternoon of May 23rd, Mr Bellinger was sipping his customary Skinny Frothy Mocha Lattechino, eating some bagel chips, and pondering the Pakflake™ brief. Mr Bellinger finished his Lattechino, looked at his desk, and found that he had not, as he had thought, been eating the bag of bagel chips, but that he had in fact accidentally munched his way through the sample box of Pakflakes™ that had been sitting next to his phone. They had been really very tasty. Mr Bellinger made a few calls. It turned out that yes, being an extruded rice and gluten compound that dissolved on contact with moisture was basically the same thing as being edible.

Mr Bellinger had an idea. He said, 'Trust me, GreenFlake, this is killer. This is going to be big,' while picking a piece of Pakflake™ out from between his teeth. None of them had any idea how big.

On June 20th the Pakflake™ campaign was launched. Sachets of spicy tomato dip were included with some products that were packed with Pakflakes™. There was also a small printed card. On it was a cartoon of a smiley-faced PakflakeTM with a speech bubble coming out of its mouth, saying: 'Yum! I'm delicious! Why not try me with salsa?'

Our records show that the first customers to encounter the new Pakflake™ promotional initiative were a Mr and Mrs Bishop of Smethwick, West Midlands. They bought a microwave oven from their local electrical shop. We believe from talking to them later that even while unpacking their microwave oven from the box, Mrs Bishop had joked about the fact that although they might have a new microwave, there wasn't actually a scrap of food in the house. Perhaps this made them more susceptible to the lure of 'why not try me with salsa?' We certainly know that the first thing that the Bishops did once they had plugged their microwave in was to heat up the salsa dip on high for 20 seconds, and then eat all the Pakflakes™ that it had come packaged with.

Then they went back to the electrical shop and bought another microwave. And ate up all those Pakflakes™ too.

Mr and Mrs Bishop bought six microwave ovens in

total that day. Apparently, by the third microwave, they were just eating the Pakflakes™ out of the box by the handful, standing in Dixons car park. They only stopped when the shop ran out of microwaves. Mr Bishop told Dixons counter staff, 'You just have to believe me, these flakes are the most delicious things I've ever eaten,' as they wrestled him to the ground outside their stock room.

By that afternoon, similar reports of spontaneous Pakflake™ gorging were coming in from all across the country. A woman in Liverpool bought twelve china figurines of Kittens At Play from a petrol station. She said she knew they were ugly but she couldn't help herself, the packaging was just so tasty. A man in Carlisle bought thirty-one nasal hair trimmers. When asked exactly what he was going to do with them all, he said, 'Get away from me! All this packaging is mine! Get your own!'

It is probably safe to say that this exceeded all of Green-Flake's customer response expectations. They sent a fax to the Federation of Polystyrene Packaging Manufacturers. It said: 'Eat this.'

Within days, there were countless reports of customers eagerly devouring the Pakflake™ packaging from their goods. There were stories of shoppers asking sales assistants which products came with Pakflakes™, and buying goods accordingly. Pollsters reported that people were buying things they didn't need, things they didn't want, and things they didn't even know how to use. Polls of shoppers reported that, frankly, people didn't care what they were buying. They were throwing the products away and keeping the packaging. GreenFlake introduced a cheesy dip for more variety. An unpacker in a large bookshop 'accidentally' got himself locked in the unpacking room one night and emerged the next morning three stone heavier, having eaten the Pakflakes™ out of three hundred and eleven boxes of Harry Potter books. At GreenFlake head office, the phones rang themselves off the walls. Orders were flooding in. They were extruding that rice-gluten compound like there was no tomorrow.

But it didn't stop there: Pakflake™ dinner-parties quickly became all the rage, with trendy young couples buying whole new sets of pots, pans and crockery, and serving up the packaging on a bed of rocket that very evening. Sides were taken in great debates as to whether one should fry or bake, roast or griddle ones Pakflakes™. Delia Smith's *Basic Pakflakery* was rushed off the presses and soon became the seminal work, leading a whole nation to stuff itself on spinach and Pakflake™ quiche, only to be supplanted days later by Nigella Lawson's *How to Be a Pakflake Goddess*. Wine buffs raged over whether the ideal accompaniment to the Pakflake™'s beguiling flavours was a new-world merlot or an old-world chardonnay. A fast-food chain tried to get in on the act by attempting to use its chicken nuggets as a packaging material, which led to a vicious courtroom ding-dong about whether stereo equipment should be resistant to saturated fats or not, and whether chicken could strictly be classed as packaging material at all. The *Daily Mail* announced that Pakflakes™ were pushing up house prices, and increasing asylum seekers. 'Now they want our flakes!' ran the headline, above a picture of some vaguely eastern European-looking men, all licking their lips.

For a while, GreenFlake tried bagging up Pakflakes™ like crisps, but they didn't sell. Surveys subsequently showed that people believed that only Pakflakes™ that had genuinely been used for packaging purposes tasted good. Pakflakes™ consumed directly in a blind-taste test were described as 'stale', 'flat-tasting', and 'kind of yucky – like eating polystyrene'. GreenFlake also tried packaging a pack of Pakflakes™ inside another pack of Pakflakes™, but for some reason, those didn't catch on either.

But these were only minor hiccups: the nation was gorging itself more and more every day. For those who really wanted maximal flakeage, the Post Office offered a book of four first-class stamps packaged in a three-foot-square box of Pakflakes™ – officially the most extreme packaging to product ratio.

Inevitably – if you could hear above the racket of all the chewing – voices of dissent could be heard. An email started doing the rounds claiming that Pakflakes™ were actually made from pork waste products, the bits that were too scraggy even to go into cheap sausages. It turned out that the source of this rumour was actually the Federation of Polystyrene Packaging Peanuts, who had been hoping to start a backlash. And a number of people did indeed become 'Flakeatarians'. There were no end of cultural critics keen to flourish the phrase 'conspicuous consumption', as though they were the first ones to have thought of it, and to go on late-night arts reviews programmes to say how they were concerned on several levels that as a society we were now so decadent that we were literally gorging ourselves on our own rubbish. One self-styled trend analyst, Joan Brownlard, went as far as to announce that what we were seeing was the snake of consumerism gorging itself on its own tail, the very death knell of capitalism itself – but as she was putting this argument forward in her own Pakflake™ diet book, her arguments all tasted a bit flat. And in any case, nobody was really listening – the country went on munching and munching and munching. Soon, localised rioting was breaking out at storage depots; delivery trucks were being hijacked. The culprits were easy enough to catch – they were always sitting at the scene of the crime, jamming handfuls of Pakflakes™ into their mouths – but even so, wasn't it all getting a bit out of control?

And then, after twelve weeks of continuous flake-related

frenzy, events took an even more unexpected turn. Ben 'Why not try me with salsa' Bellinger, arguably the man responsible for lighting the touch-paper of the whole Pakflake™ phenomenon, was found dead at the GreenFlake Industries extruding plant in Bracknell. The autopsy recorded Death By Misadventure, the misadventure being that of sticking his mouth over the end of one of the main extruding nozzles and trying to eat the raw Pakflake™ mixture. Even if Mr Bellinger hadn't exploded, the autopsy concluded, the levels of gluten in his body were highly toxic.

Suddenly, the taste of Pakflakes™ soured on the nation's tongues. As news of the Bracknell Misadventure spread, people started spitting out the flakes in disgust. What had we been doing? Were we mad? The man who brought Pakflakes™? to the nation had exploded? What had happened to us? And anyway, what the hell were we going to do with nine microwaves, thirteen mobile phones and seven copies of *How to be a Pakflake Goddess*?

And as the nation wiped its chin, rinsed out its mouth and sucked peppermints to take the taste away, the Federation of Polystyrene Packaging Manufacturers issued a statement: In these times of renewed sobriety, they said, what was needed was a more traditional packaging peanut. A packaging peanut you could rely on. And they, the Federation of Polystyrene Packaging Peanut Manufacturers, were here to provide such a thing. You didn't think we'd be back? they said. Why, that really sticks in our throats.

THANK YOU for visiting www.remembertheflake.com. Click here to tell a friend. Click here to log off.

* * *

So close

HE IS having one of his nervous days, where he flinches at litter and everything worries him. They are standing at the bus shelter. Stop fidgeting, she says. In this city you are never more than six feet away from a rat, he says. He is wringing his hands, twisting them round one another like knotting worms.

That night in bed, as he once again sleeps with his head on her belly, she closes her eyes tight and wills her skin to become transparent. In a moment she will open her eyes again, and if she has gone see-through, she will smile, and then wake him, and say – look! Your face is but two inches away from my shit! Look at it lying there silently, curled up inside me!

* * *

the shortage at the petting zoo

TIMES BEING what they are, we have found it increasingly difficult to get hold of what you might call normal farm animals. Disease has done for the sheep. Goats are only to be found on the black market. And cows – you think we'd let children anywhere near the cows since our falling-out with the air ambulance? Old Lomax the donkey still struggles on, but what with the volume of children we have to contend with, it gets a bit much for him. He's sensitive to their scornful glances. And you have to see it from their side: they were having to queue for forty minutes, and even then they could only scratch his ears if they wore protective gloves.

So we have had to explore more unorthodox supply options: From the cockroaches, the children learn the importance of teamwork; from the puffa fish they learn tolerance of others, plus a basic understanding of toxicology; the hyenas seem to foster sharing, as well as lightning-fast reactions. They are also responsible for an unexpected increase in reading age. The fountainhead crab is highly effective in improving the children's posture.

We have also seen a general improvement in good manners and helpfulness to others, although we cannot say for certain whether this comes from the horned sea slugs or the baby cobras. And how the wasps have helped the youngsters with their tidying-away skills, we cannot say.

Tomorrow we take delivery of an alligator, which we have managed to secure via an insider at the big zoo. We're very excited. We have a number of workshops planned.

the minister for defence forgets

IT TRANSPIRES that I am the Minister for Defence. I am once again pondering this fact on a flight back to Heathrow. In my briefcase is a dossier, written by my own hand, which is concerned with the various details of the day-to-day requirements of being a Minister: colleagues' names; where to find the Parliament buildings; which laws are just and which are unjust; and so forth. I have just finished a very successful meeting with the American fellows. They have various 'sectors' which they consider to be 'ripe' for 'expansion'. I concurred wholeheartedly with their sentiment. I even added a few comments of my own about the general 'favourability' of the 'climate'. They seemed pleased. We all shook hands and then they showed me to my limousine. As my car pulled away and headed for the airport, I looked back and saw them all nodding to each other in a satisfied way, the way you would on the step of a restaurant after a particularly fine meal.

I had been careful not to mention that for the last six months I have been suffering from a profound amnesia, and have completely forgotten everything I might have once known about being Minister for Defence. I have also forgotten most other things, for that matter, such as whether I have a wife and family, where I might live, who we are currently at war with and who we are not currently at war with. I have retained, for some reason, the information that I am a shoe size seven, which is forty-one in European measurements.

I must have known somehow that the amnesia was on its way, or why else would I have prepared such detailed notes?

Perhaps the amnesia came on slowly? I used to lie in a sweat at night worrying about this, until one day I realised that one more unanswered question when my mind was already so foggy was really not going to make one jot of difference. So now I approach the question of the origin of my amnesia as a philosophical one, to be taken out on long train journeys or international flights, and turned over in my mind by way of a distraction, like those puzzles you get in a cracker, where you have to try to twist apart two bent bits of wire.

It seems certain from my notes that before I forgot everything, I had a family. I have written nothing to indicate what sort of family we were, whether we were close or distant, loving or brittle. I do not appear to have left myself any details about how to get in touch with them, so I hesitantly draw the conclusion that they have taken the opportunity of my forgetting to quietly slip away. In the absence of any evidence either way, I have decided to treat this as the best thing that could have happened, in the circumstances. Sometimes I imagine the children that I might or might not have: a girl with beautiful long hair and a special smile for her daddy, a girl who is doing well with her flute playing and hopes to make the orchestra next year; a boy who has been difficult perhaps, but after a stint in a Saturday job has come round and is now doing well. I hope that he misses me most of all. My wife. I wonder what she is like? For some reason, I do not have the energy for even an imaginary wife.

My notes say that I must press hard in the cause of *expansion*. I have underlined it in several places. In order for sufficient opportunities for *growth* (there's another underlined word), there must be expansion in the various *sectors*. Can we really go on expanding forever? It doesn't seem feasible. Can't we just stay the same, perhaps move things around a bit? I look at my colleagues and think, does this obsession with expansion come from spending too much time staring at their own bellies?

I have begun inviting the brightest students from the political colleges to visit me in my offices. I say to them: assume that I know nothing whatsoever. Explain the war to me. The students intuit at once that this is probably some kind of test, or else perhaps a display of highly distilled cynicism on my part. They will usually start out by explaining the *factors*. I say that surely, nobody ever went to war over *factors*. Then perhaps they will try and tell me about the *context*. This is always interesting, and I frequently take notes. Where did the warring sides get their weapons? I might ask. From us, the students might reply. Then is the war not our fault? I ask. No, no, the students reply. The blame for the war lies with the warring parties. How are we to halt the war? I ask. At this point the students will either explain patiently that the war in question is not our fault, and so putting a stop to it isn't something that we need to consider, or else they will embark on a lengthy dissertation about different manners of political pressure. I try to keep up, but invariably they'll lose me. Under the desk I'll slip off my shoes, and put them back on again. I'll nod periodically and they'll stumble on. Eventually I'll smile, and they'll look relieved, and I'll tell them thank you, in a way that might imply that, if this situation were some kind of test, then they have probably passed it.

When things get a bit much, I go to a shoe shop. The shop assistant will say, what size, sir? And I will reply with confidence: a size seven please. That's a forty-one. When the shoes arrive I'll slip my feet into them and walk up and down a bit, admiring them in those little mirrors they have at ankle height. 'Are they comfortable?' the shopkeeper will ask.

'Oh they are. Most certainly,' I'll reply.

* * *

knots familiar to donald crowhurst

Running knots.
Bowline knots.
Miller's knots.
Stopper knots.
Stomach knots.

* * *

the year of weeping

SPRING: AROUND Leah, I cry a lot. And we're not just talking about any old 'bursting into tears' here – no, we're talking an uncontrollable weeping that can go on for hours at a time. The slightest thing about her can set me off. On our first date, as we sat in the restaurant making nervous small talk, I was suddenly overtaken by a sense of the infinite beauty of the shape of her ear. And with that, I started sobbing. The tears ran in sheets down my face. The paper table-cloth turned to mush. My shirt was drenched. Soon I was sobbing so hard I could barely catch my breath. It was something of a shock, I can tell you. Unfazed by this unexpected turn of events, Leah simply gathered up extra napkins from the tables all around and we eventually managed to stem the flooding.

Later, back at hers, as she dabbed at my blotchy face with the largest bath towel she could find, I mumbled what apologies I could. She told me not to worry, that it was rare to find a man who could let it all out like that, and then she kissed me and silently undressed me and all was going well until I caught a glimpse of her bare shoulder in the moonlight, and I was off again. Don't worry, she said, holding me tight, imagine we're making love in a rainstorm. I kissed my tears from where they were landing on her breasts and she shielded her eyes from the worst of the torrent, and afterwards we lay side by side in silence, listening to the rat-a-tat of my teardrops on the wooden floor.

Even with the inconvenience of my strange new affliction, we do just fine. We simply make sure there are plenty of buckets and sponges on hand in every room, and when we make love, I screw my eyes up tight and try to think arid thoughts. Leah says she doesn't see me as being different to any other man. I tell her how lucky I am to have her. She usually says nothing, just smiles and strokes my damp cheek.

SUMMER: Recently, Leah did the sweetest thing. I had accidentally caught sight of her thigh as she walked across the lounge in her dressing gown. Before I could even shout a warning, my eyes were squirting like water pistols. Leah turned and seemed to hesitate for a second, and then she took a little glass bottle – I suppose you could call it a phial – out of her dressing gown pocket and handed it to me.

'Catch a few drops in this, would you, Edward? We should keep some you know. This weeping won't go on for ever, and in a funny kind of way, we'll miss it when it's gone.'

I did as she said. When the little phial was full, she took it from me, screwed the top on tightly and put it back in her pocket.

AUTUMN: I suppose it would be fair to say that these days, things aren't what they used to be. It seems that Leah now finds my weeping rather tiresome. It's the withering look and the way she spits 'Oh, belt up, cry-baby' that gives it away. Nevertheless, she still seems keen to catch a few of my tears in her little brown phials, so I suppose that counts for something. In fact, sometimes I'll be sitting, minding my own business, and Leah will hand me a phial even when I'm not actually crying, and then, before I can say anything, she'll have flashed me a look at the curve of her neck, or shown me her knee, and I'll be off. She has been known to do this as many as half a dozen times a day. If I'm honest, it can get pretty draining. It leaves me with a crashing headache and a terrible craving for ready-salted crisps. I tell myself I should be grateful though. What other woman would want a cry-baby around the house?

WINTER: Leah now just leaves me with a box of glass phials and a stack of Polaroid pictures that she's taken of herself: the curve of her belly; the line of her calf; neck meets collarbone; left breast seen from the side; closed eye while sleeping. Leah seems to spend most of her time going to the post office, or else taking herself off shopping. I sit and look at the photographs and give myself up to the involuntary torrents. Today, however, I flicked through the stack of photographs a dozen times, but no tears came. It was something of a surprise. I got up to make myself a cup of tea, and that's how I found it. Leah must have left it by accident on the kitchen side. It was one of the little brown phials, full of tears and with the lid sealed shut. But there was also a sticky label on the bottle. The print was small but clearly legible. It said: 'Genuine Man Tears. 25ml. Cried freely, without the aid of alcohol or sport. Very rare. One drop, nightly, on the pillows of your male-born children, will soften their sensibilities. £34.99.'

My eyes start to sting. But differently this time. I doubt Leah will be wanting to bottle any of these.

* * *

The people next door

We've been invited to supper by the people next door. It's a bit awkward: we don't call it supper, we call it 'tea'. Though technically tea-time is about half five-ish, whereas we imagine supper is probably eight-ish, and more likely to involve wine. Also, the people next door are cannibals.

* * *

Portrait of a Life Gleaned From the Template Text Messages on a Nokia 7360

I'm in a meeting.
Call me later.
I'm busy right now.
I'll call you later.
Meeting is cancelled.
I am late.
Please call.
Happy Birthday.
I love you too.
See you?
I am late.
I'll call you later.

* * *

a clarification

THE DOORS were never intended to open. They were there strictly for decoration. And we're sorry you barged through them, but we're quite squeamish, so you'll just have to remove the splinters yourself.

* * *

the belgian copper crisis of 1976

SO A FRIEND of mine said that she was having a plumber round to fix her boiler, which had taken to turning itself on during heatwaves. I said that by way of small talk, she might mention the Belgian Copper Crisis of 1976. It's always good to show a bit of insider knowledge, I said. Shows them you mean business, that it's no good trying to pull the wool over your eyes. Knowing about the Belgian Copper Crisis is your ticket to courteous and efficient service when it comes to plumbers, I said. She seemed keen to know more, so I told her:

In 1976, for reasons that are now forgotten, there was an unforseen Europe-wide shortage of copper. Spare parts were scarce, but new pipes were even rarer. In a desperate attempt to fill demand, builders started sourcing ready-made copper pipes from Belgium. Thin-walled pipes and thick-walled pipes, couplings, flanges and T-junctions – in 1976 they were all Belgian. New houses were going up all that summer with Belgian copper laced right through them.

By the winter of 1976 everything was fine again, and copper from the usual sources was available once more.

Now for reasons best known only to themselves, Belgian pipe sizes are non-standard. They're not compatible with any other country in Europe. Not that the Belgians seem to care. Perhaps it's because they're self-sufficient in copper? Which means that there are houses out there whose pipes, fitted in that sweltering summer of 1976, are the absolute bane of plumbers' lives. They're impossible to get parts for. If you're unlucky enough to own a house built in 1976, then your address is passed round from plumber to plumber, via noticeboards in hardware stores, scribbled on grubby bits of paper kept on the dashboards of white vans, and posted up on secret plumber websites. Ever had a problem getting a plumber to come and look at your leaky radiator? Then you have Belgian pipes. I guarantee it.

My friend said she appreciated this information. She said she would mention it. I was happy to help. It's always awkward when a tradesman is working away in your house and you've got nothing else to say other than 'Would you like a cup of tea?'

Before she went, I reminded her that, although it is now known as the 'Belgian Copper Crisis', the Belgians themselves were not the ones with the crisis. In fact they did rather well out of the whole episode. She said yes, she understood.

It was only later, as I recalled the look of gratitude on her face, that it occurred to me that there were a few details about the Belgian Copper Crisis of 1976 about which I was not entirely clear:

a) I wasn't entirely sure that it happened in 1976.

b) I couldn't be absolutely certain that the metal in question was copper.

c) I was also in some doubt as to whether it actually involved the Belgians.

Still, I felt that the gist of the story seemed to ring a definite bell. I'll text my friend tonight and see how it went down.

the horse killer

THE HORSES are bitter and brittle animals, and we long ago gave up trying to ride them. They cluster on the plains like restless shadows. We watch them from the rocky outcrops. When a herd is of a mind to canter, they move like an unruly tide, ebbing in improbable ways. At these times we keep our distance. The snorting and the rumble of hooves make the air quake so much that the rocky outcrops become unsafe places. We worry about being shaken off. And while we cling to the trees as the ground rolls and trembles with the horses' thunder, we also worry about how we have perhaps failed ourselves: what is wrong with us that our horses are so wild and angry? We imagine that across the hills, the other tribes are using their horses to pull their traps to church, or pull their ploughs, or to be petted by their children.

On the last day of summer, the Horse Killer carries out his duty. He takes his Horse Hammer and walks out onto the plain. The horses know him instantly, and snort and whinny, and rear up on their hind legs, thrashing their front hooves in the air. The Horse Killer says that when they do this, the air whistles through their fetlocks and makes terrible screeching sounds. The Horse Killer will select the horse he wants, and set off at a jog to confront it. The herd know what is to come, and make way for the Horse Killer. The horse who has been selected knows its fate, too, and bolts.

But the Horse Killer is swift and strong. He has trained all year for this. The horses, for all their bitterness, know when they are beaten, and usually turn to face the Horse Killer and their fate. Then the Horse Killer will raise his hammer and strike.

And due to their brittleness, the horse will shatter into a thousand pieces. The herd will frenzy, and the Horse Killer will be trampled as they flood their way across the plain.

We move silently in their wake, and collect the horse-shards in bags and buckets. We separate these shards into sizes. Usually, we select a shard the size of a fist which is fashioned into a goblet. We use this as a drinking vessel at the ceremony at which we will choose the new Horse Killer. The largest shard will then be presented to him, to fashion into his hammer.

As the new Horse Killer begins to carve his hammer, the stallions on the plain gallop in circles, whipping up a dust storm that blots out the stars.

* * *

fragments from the history of pest control

No 1: R A B B I T S
This is how we keep the rabbits under control. At night, when they are asleep in their hutches and holes, we creep out and, using the megaphones that are made for the amplifying of whispers, we sidle up to their sleeping places and whisper to them.

We whisper that they are beautiful. We whisper that they should look at themselves and see this. Regard how beguiling you look in the moonlight, you rabbits, we say. See how you cast such a fine shadow on the earth. Stop your rabbiting around and regard! Those sure are fine shadows. Just look!

But these are not kind words that we are saying, and we don't say them out of love or generosity. We speak them because we know that rabbits are vain, the vainest of all the animals. We speak it because we know that when they get up on the moonlit nights and go about their mischief, that something in their rabbity brains will remember the words that we have spoken, and they will stop, and look at their shadows cast on the ground, and they will think, I am indeed a very fine rabbit, oh yes. And they will continue staring, beguiled by their own shadow, mesmerised by their own seeming beauty. And they will stay like this for just ages.

Which is when we are able to step from the other shadows with our sticks.

No 2: B I R D S

Instances of hair-stealing have been on the increase, that we will admit. Children have been targeted.

An educational programme has been set in motion, warning of the dangers of birds. Posters have been printed and displayed prominently in schools, drawing attention to the roles of beaks, talons, etc. in the hair-stealing process. There is a helpline which can be called. Please believe us that we are working flat out to develop anti-bird hair. However, until such a time as this becomes available, we are advising the following:

a) The handing over of all hair if challenged by birds. (Carry your own scissors in order to facilitate hair removal.)

b) The wearing of hats (mild deterrent), or

c) The wearing of wigs (baffling to the birds, escape is sometimes possible in the confusion).

d) The cutting off of all hair (renders theft irrelevant).

Some birds (doves, hummingbirds, ones which can produce character references) will be exempt from the new anti-bird policies. Some hairstyles will be declared provocative to birds, and require special licensing. Please see notices in salons for status updates.

No 3: F R O G S

The frogs have louche and intelligent eyes. They have taken to lounging around in the manner of cats. They mutter and yawn and turn away when approached, affecting indifference and belching offhand croaks of superiority. We find them disgusting, which makes our work easier.

Their superior attitude will be their undoing. We have begun to tempt them with the choicest baits: cryptic conundrums, puzzles and codes, esoteric philosophies and abstruse ontologies and all manner of morsels irresistible to their intellectual snobbery. Only yesterday a number of frogs were overheard arguing about an anagram we had left by the pond. It will soon be possible for us to act.

Oh, you affected frogs, your days are numbered.

No 4: W A L R U S E S

For the longest time the antics of the walruses were highly comical to us. The way they would sit around on those rocks, basking their fat sausagey bodies in the sun and barking all over the place. The way they jostled each other for position like grumpy old women on buses, the way they dived for fish with their ridiculous belly flops. And all the time that barking! It made us laugh!

We don't mind admitting that they had us fooled for quite a while. All the time we thought they were just clowning around, they were really just biding their time. Then one day they swarmed into the town and took over all the underground passageways — the tube lines, the sewage pipes, the ducts and access tunnels. People were angry! The barks of the walruses amplified through the pipes, and it was like the earth itself was mocking us with a sort of drunken carping. There was a terrible smell of fish. People were frightened.

Sometimes we lower ourselves into the tunnels on ropes, and play our torches across the underground seas of blinking walrus eyes. It is at these times that we are aware of how badly we've misjudged them. There is a danger in the air. Something is definitely afoot. Though we must say that their fat sausagey bodies still look pretty dumb to us.

We wish to make amends for our previous poor judgement, but all our methods are proving ineffective. Now we are hearing rumours of elephant seals massing in the north. The smell of fish has become almost intolerable. We fear that time may be running out, and that apologies may be in order.

No 5: T R E E S

We shoot trees. This is how it has always been done. Recently, we have begun to question our methods. Trees are not, we concede, difficult targets — they cannot run nor dodge, and they have never given us cause to use our telescopic sights or laser-guidance features.

And often, as we watch them crack and shred and splinter under the barrage of our automatic fire, we realise that we cannot ignore that all around us, under our feet and in the forests, shoots and saplings are pushing their way towards the sunlight, and all our efforts feel so futile.

* * *

the boyle curriculum

MONDAY. The morning lessons had gone badly. Somehow our topic on 'families' had been side-tracked by little Tony Docherty who claimed that his older brother was a hijacker, which had made some of the other children cry. I knew full well that Tony Docherty's older brother was in fact a steeplejack, and tried to get things under control by asking if anyone in the class could tell me what a chimney was for, but the children had just looked at me blankly. I'm ashamed to say that I deducted 76 house points for their ignorance, and from there the lesson degenerated into squabbling and name-calling. I think we all said things we regretted.

In the afternoon, I had the children take down the posters that covered our walls — even the one which showed how all smokers were bad on the inside — and I had them stick up large sheets of plain black rice paper instead. Then we all sat down in the story circle in our newly blacked-out classroom, and I began to tell the class about my brother, Boyle.

'What kind of man is my brother Boyle?' I said. The children listened without a whisper. 'My brother Boyle is the kind of man who, if you rushed to him in a panic because your house was on fire, would make a great show of lending you his smallest bucket. You would snatch it from his hand and use it to try and douse the fire-storm that was engulfing your home, but all the time what you'd really be worried about would be the safe return of his puny bucket.'

The children were wide-eyed with concern. I continued:

'And also, for years afterwards, you would have to endure Boyle telling others how he had practically saved you from the flames single-handedly. You would have to sit there at his dinner-parties as he slapped his enormous thigh and boomed to his wife Lorraine across the table: "If it wasn't for me, my little brother would be nothing but soot by now!" And you would have to sit there and smile and agree and say yes, it's true, Boyle practically snuffed out the flames with his own bare hands, and in fact, it's a travesty he hasn't been decorated for bravery, or been asked to give the benefit of his wisdom to our emergency services .'

The children sat in silence for some moments. Then Peter Mathers put his hand up and asked exactly what volume of fluid a 'puny bucket' could be expected to hold. I said, 'about a chimneyful', which shut him up.

TUESDAY. This morning the children quietly got on with drawing pictures of burning houses. I had to send Tony Docherty over to 3C in the next portacabin along to ask if we could borrow some of their red and yellow crayons, as we had worn all of ours down to little stubs. Once the children had filled their exercise books, they started on the black paper. Their enthusiastic red and yellow inferno was an impressive sight, and the children seemed pleased with their handiwork. I awarded extra house points all round.

Come the afternoon, the children sat themselves cross-legged in the story circle without any prompting. Mary spoke on behalf of them: 'Sir,' she said, 'we're not sure we understand yet. Tell us more about what kind of man Boyle is.'

So I told them: 'What kind of a man is my brother Boyle? My brother Boyle is the kind of man who, if you telephoned him for advice because you had found a tiny, injured bird in your garden, would come straight round and hit it with a shovel. You would stand in shock for a minute, as the deathly clang echoed around you, and then all of a sudden you would feel ashamed of yourself that you didn't have his no-nonsense attitude to the circle of life. You would vow to learn to light fires with flint, to skin rabbits with sharpened sticks, and to apologise to Boyle at once for being such a spineless ditherer compared to him.

'Then later, while you were cleaning bits of baby sparrow off your patio, you would learn that he'd told his beautiful wife Lorraine that if she wanted his opinion, the poor little creature would probably have survived, if only it had been scooped up and kept in a shoebox and fed bits of milky bread, but that he, Boyle, knew that his little brother would not have had the patience for such things, so he'd just done his grim duty with a heavy heart. And the next time you saw Lorraine, you would be able to do nothing more than cringe and turn away, thinking all the while that you could hear her whisper "bird killer" under her breath.'

After I'd finished, we looked up sparrows in our Bumper Book of Ornithology. Peter Mathers asked: 'Sir, what is the circumference of the circle of life?' but I pretended not to hear him and busied myself getting out the craft box, and we spent the rest of the afternoon making little model birds. In almost no time at all the children fashioned the most incredible array of delicate creatures. They folded tissue paper into tiny pointed beaks and made claws out of finely tweaked drinking straws. The intricacy of the feathers was a marvel, especially given the blunt safety-scissors they were working with. Some of the models looked uncannily lifelike, perched on the ends of the desks, and the children role-played nurturing them and feeding them crumbs from their hands.

Under my instruction, Tony Docherty then role-played being Boyle, and, using an exercise book Sellotaped onto a metre ruler as his shovel, he stomped around the classroom shouting: 'It's all for the best!' and smashed the birds to bits with great angry shovel-swipes.

In no time, our entire classroom was a scene of devastation: smashed tissue birds were everywhere, and many of the children were crying. The only bird still intact belonged to Peter Mathers. Peter's bird was an engineering marvel: a complex lattice of several dozen straws, and hundreds of finely folded sheets of tissue paper. It had a wing-span of nearly two feet. Tony Docherty strode over to it and raised his metre-rule shovel and shouted 'circle of life!' but at the very last second Peter snatched the bird away and flung it out of the window. We all stood transfixed as it glided up into the air, flew higher than the school, and then with what I could have sworn was a flap of its tissue wings, soared away over the sports hall.

Before the home-time bell went, I handed out the Boyle Worksheets. These contained multiple-choice questions concerning the many subtle cruelties of Boyle. I hoped it would help the children further their understanding.

WEDNESDAY. Today we spent most of the day preparing for the Boyle Musical, which we will perform as the end-of-term show. I am going to write songs for the children to sing, so that the catchy tunes will lodge forever in their heads, reminding them how pompous, vain, deceitful Boyle is. The children worked hard on a pair of enormous papier-maché heads of Boyle and Lorraine for the show. Even rendered in mushed-up newspaper and poster-paints the likenesses were quite striking. At intervals I'd shout out, 'What kind of man is Boyle?' and the children would shout back, 'He is the kind of man who would sell your coat on the internet and then drag you on a long winter walk so he could laugh at what a funny shade of blue you went', or some other fact from the Boyle Worksheets.

At one point, I left the classroom for a few minutes to photocopy some song-sheets, and when I returned I saw that the children had raided my supply of gold stars that I use for awarding house-points, and had stuck them in the hair of the papier-maché Lorraine-head. I suppose I should have been cross, but the way the little stars shimmered and sparkled in the afternoon light was quite stunning. I reached out a hand, part of me expecting her hair to feel real and lustrous to my touch. I said: 'Children, gather round and see what kind of a woman Lorraine is. See how beautiful she is.' The children gathered round. We counted the stars in her hair. There were one hundred and twenty-six. So that's how many extra house points I awarded the class.

THURSDAY. Today, when the children come in, I tell them to keep their hats and coats on, as we're going on a field trip. A Boyle field trip. I hand out clipboards and binoculars and we all bundle into the school mini-bus and drive to Boyle's house. When we arrive I tell the children to form a crocodile and stay low, and follow me, and we sneak along the perimeter wall to the large oak tree. I tell the children that from the topmost branches we will get an excellent view of Boyle's house, and we all clamber up, the bigger children helping the smaller ones. I say that I am very impressed with their team-work as we all find perches among the branches and leaves. We secure our clipboards and the children focus their binoculars and begin to scan the grounds.

The children say: 'Boyle certainly seems like the kind of man to have a very big house. It is very grand and well-kept. There are twenty-seven chimneys.'

I say: 'I think what you mean is that it's unnecessarily large, showy, ostentatious. Make sure you write that down.'

The children look again and say: 'We can also see orchards and horses grazing on the lawns!'

I say: 'Boyle is the kind of man who knows his little brother is terrified of horses, yet has them roaming free on his land. Write that down.'

Then the children say: 'Also, we can see that standing on the front step is a very beautiful woman. She has long yellow hair and pale skin and even though she is frowning and seems to be pointing in this direction in an angry manner, she shines like she is lit by a thousand tiny stars!'

'Lorraine!' I say, snatching a pair of binoculars out of Mary Tranter's hands. 'Oh, Lorraine! Write this down: how can my brother Boyle ever appreciate what a perfect creature his wife is? If she were my wife I'd never leave her side. If she were my wife I'd spend every day gazing into those beautiful eyes and stroking her shining hair. My brother Boyle is the kind of man who does not deserve such a wife.'

The children say: 'Wow. She really is beautiful, isn't she? Can we get any closer?'

I say: 'Perhaps after dark.'

Mary Tranter says: 'Sir, how do you spell "restraining order"?'

And then Peter Mathers shouts 'Look!', and we all look up in the air to where he is pointing, and see that from out of the clouds is gliding his tissue-paper bird. It swoops round the tree, its paper wings burring, and then continues on its way, gliding towards one of Boyle's chimney-tops. Suddenly I find myself in the grip of a terrible anger, and I thrash my way up through the branches to the very top of the tree, and leap desperately at the bird.

I grab it mid-wing-beat. As I fall, I see the children scribbling furiously on their clipboards. I can hear sirens. By the time I hit the ground I have torn the bird to shreds.

FRIDAY. The children will probably be having a supply teacher around now. I wonder what kind of supply teacher the supply teacher will be?

* * *

why the national anthem turned out rubbish

Are you the composer of the National Anthem?

Yes, I am.

Well, it's rubbish. Sixty-eight verses and no rhyming – what were you thinking? And in a minor key, too. This will really depress people. Morale could be threatened, you know.

Yes, I am sorry. But everyone was knackered after helping build the city wall. The authorities were desperate. Also, I lied on my CV and said I could play the banjo.

* * *

the muteness of things
To accompany an exhibition of still life paintings by Tadeusz Deregowski

Extract from E F Walser's Forgotten Folk Tales:
ONCE UPON a time there was an artist who was endowed with a terrible gift – when he painted a portrait, it revealed the innermost secrets of the subject to all who looked upon it. The artist, being a fellow of good conscience (but also unable to stop himself painting, for that was his destiny), devised a strategy. If anyone wanted their portrait painting, he would say to them: 'I will happily paint your picture. But on one condition. You may look at it yourself, but you must never, ever show it to anyone else.' People were happy to agree to these terms, as they knew that they would learn much from looking at his painting of themselves: one's innermost secrets are, after all, rarely known to oneself. And the artist entered into this pact of secrecy with the highest of motives: by looking at his paintings, he felt, they would be able to live better, happier lives. And so, he was able to continue painting, and people's secrets stayed hidden, and not out in the world where they could cause upset and havoc. He was the most celebrated artist in the land, despite the fact that no one had ever seen anything he had painted.

One winter's day, however, when the weather was cold and no one had come to his studio to request a picture for many days, the artist decided to paint a self-portrait. He set up a mirror and his easel and mixed his paints, and began tracing the outline of his own features. He worked on the picture for several days. As he worked he was pleased – his brush-strokes were unusually keen, the likeness was, he had to admit, exceptionally good. But when the painting was dry and he looked upon it again, it told him a terrible secret: it told him that in his heart of hearts, he didn't enter into the pact of secrecy with his subjects in order to protect them – he did it because he liked the feeling of having wriggled like woodworm into their lives. He liked the fact that all over the land, people couldn't help peeking at pictures of themselves, and either saying a small prayer of thanks to him, or muttering dark words of hatred.

The artist was greatly distressed by this revelation, and smashed his easel, stamped on his paints so that they burst all over his feet, and resolved never to paint again. After several anguished days, however, he realised that as long as he was alive, he couldn't keep himself from painting. So instead of portraits, from this day forward, he told himself, he would paint only still lives: vases of flowers, tiny ornaments, arrangements of bottles. Never again would he paint a human face. Never again would he unwittingly reveal a secret.

The artist painted his bottles, flowers, ornaments. for just a few months before, quite unexpectedly one blustery evening, he was killed at his easel as he worked on a painting. A rich merchant, suspecting his wife of infidelity, had found a miniature that the artist had painted of her. And on looking at the portrait, he saw instantly that his wife had not in fact been unfaithful to him, but that her heart harboured something much worse: in truth, she had never loved the merchant, she found him ignorant, and had married him out of a mixture of pity and greed. Unable to take out his rage on his wife, whom he loved, he sought out the artist, and stabbed him through the heart. He then took the paintings that were hanging around the studio, the paintings of bottles and flowers and ornaments, and flung them into the river.

It is said that the paintings floated away, and have turned up over time at all four corners of the globe. It is also said that you can tell them instantly: they are strange and unsettling to look at. Because although the artist never again revealed the secrets of another human subject after the day he painted his self-portrait, his terrible gift was still at work: the bottles, ornaments, fruit, and so on. – all these inanimate objects are also full of secrets. But they speak in a language we cannot understand. The effect of seeing one of these paintings, saturated as it is with the whisperings of objects, is said to be upsetting in ways that hang just out of reach, like a sneeze that never quite comes. The world of objects, it seems, is a frightening and unpleasant place. We should be thankful we do not have to learn what they really know. We are saved only from this knowledge by the muteness of things.

– E F Walser, 1923

IT IS EASY to see why this story ended up in *Forgotten Folk Tales*. Speaking frankly, it is an opportunity squandered. Walser clearly thought so too – his unpublished papers contain some 700 additional pages of notes concerning this one story alone, many of them being his own elaborations and imaginings of the lives of those who had their portraits painted. (As with many of the tales collected in Walser's volume, one gets the distinct impression that he saw these strange directionless failures as almost his responsibility. He desperately wanted to help them 'come good'.) On several occasions he calls 'The Artist's Tale' 'the tale that went awry'. The artist, after all, should have been a minor figure, a catalyst as it were, in a grander piece. Who cares, really, for the fine morals of painters? Especially one who seems to regard portraiture somewhat pompously as a mere branch of self-help. And who wants to read about well-kept secrets, anyway? And just as we get down to some interesting stuff, we veer off into some hokum about creepy ornaments. No! We want more in the rich merchant vein: love, money, greed, deceit, violence of certain types, beautiful women with dark secrets in their hearts. Just generally more about beautiful women, if we're honest.

Why then is it reproduced here? Let me just say this: I visited Tadeusz Deregowski's rented flat in North London in the winter of 2003 to look at some fine monoprints he had made. While he was in the kitchen, searching for a second wine glass, I fell to perusing his bookcase. Mr Deregowski did not have a copy of *Forgotten Folk Tales*. Indeed, as I was to learn later, nobody does – but he did have a well-thumbed edition of Hasselmann's *Objects, Dreams, Terrors*. I dimly remembered that Hasselmann had been a disciple of Jung, but that the two had had some kind of falling-out after Hasselmann had penned a drinking song parodying Jung's theory of archetypes. I took the book down from the shelf, but before I could turn to the biographical note to check my recollection of its author's infamy, a folded piece of paper fell out from between its covers. I unfolded it. It was a photocopy of 'The Artist's Tale'. Feeling somehow that I had come across something that Deregowski would not have wished me to see, I quickly read the extract. There were angry-seeming jottings in the margins. Just as I was tilting the page this way and that, trying to decipher the scrawl (was it Deregowski's? I could not tell), there was an exclamation from down the hall. A second glass! Hastily, I folded the Walser tale up, and slipped it back between the pages of Hasselmann, and returned the book to the shelf.

What it means to Deregowski I cannot say. Although what it says about these paintings, with their lurking sense of menace, we can perhaps guess. Perhaps you could ask him about it now, though I suspect he will deny ever having owned such a thing as a work by Hasselmann. For myself, after leaving

Deregowski's flat that night, with Walser's tale buzzing in my head, my life was never quite the same again. I was intrigued by the existence of such a thing as a book of forgotten folk tales. My search for Walser's work had all manner of unexpected effects on my life. But that is another story entirely – one that contains more than enough money, greed, deceit, violence of certain types, and not nearly enough love nor beautiful women. No beautiful women at all, if I'm honest.

* * *

storage

A YOUNG couple come most Wednesdays. She's Japanese, he's... I don't know, just sort of undifferentiated male. They always bring with them just one item: a parcel, about the size of a shoebox, neatly wrapped in brown paper. The unit is in her name. She always completes all the details meticulously in the signing-in book, which everybody else usually ignores. The sign on the wall above the signing-in book says that the information is required from patrons in accordance with 'Correct Fire Procedure'. Everyone knows that in case of fire the correct procedure is just to run away from the fire.

The man looks kind of listless, and she looks kind of ferocious in a compact, focused sort of way, like she's being vigilant against some kind of attack. I watch them on the camera as they access their unit: she stands in various postures of mild annoyance, holding the brown paper-wrapped parcel as he fumbles for the keys to their padlock.

I imagine that she is neurotically fastidious and that their two-bedroom flat is the epitome of arid minimalism. I imagine that she is constantly berating the man for various transgressions concerning small domestic matters: incorrect placement of teaspoons in the cutlery tray; alignments of DVDs on a shelf; poor efforts in folding jumpers in the drawer, etc. I imagine an Excel spreadsheet at the heart of their lives, stipulating correct procedure for all activities in their lives. I imagine brittle silences and half-concealed heavy sighs deployed with devastating accuracy just at the edge of his earshot. I imagine that she uses a double-feint concerning her perceived cultural stereotype of the Japanese as an ordered, meticulous people, in order to get away with what is, largely, just bad-tempered control-freakery.

I imagine that the packages contain boxes full of postcards, on which she makes him write short essays confessing his various failings. When a box is full, they bring them here, to the facility.

What will happen when their unit is finally full of boxes?

Like everyone else, they will get a bigger unit.

* * *

found report:
idea for a photon cannon

THE number of times my rogue has had attacks parried or dodged from behind their target while in stealth never happened. Got it? That's because you didn't position yourself right! If you stand inside the mob or too close, your weapons can go through it, and you will get Lord of the Rings Online Gold parried, etc.

This idea Kerrigan had against heavy units came after she witnessed Terran Armor Annihilators tear through some Ultalisks very easily. This fly for fun penya new member of the swarm was engineered directly towards eliminating heavy units. The only drawback is to the Protoss with Twilight Archons. However, since the Infiltratorlisk jumps inside and tears a hole then destroys the heavy unit would mean that the Infiltratorlisk could be used against Immortals, evening things up with the Armor Annihilator not being able to attack Immortals but could attack Twilight Archons.

Well. That's my Zerg unit for my heavy unit counter idea. I hope you enjoy. This unit would be the protoss equivalent to the Armor Annihilator and the Infiltratorlisk. The Hyper Destroyer would be mechanical and would fire from one photon cannon at the top. However, this photon cannon wouldn't be a photon cannon, it would be a charged buy weapon to fire at enemy heavy units. It would take about 3-5 seconds for the weapon to get fully charged. During those three seconds a large ball of deadly energy will mass in front of the photon cannon then after 3-5 seconds will fire, doing much more fly for fun penya damage in one blow, but taking more time. Since this cannon takes a while to use, small units will be able to overpower it easily, as all that power is used on only 1 unit where it isn't necessary. The Hyper Destroyers cannon activates Immortals shields so it is not useful. Seeing that Terrans and Zerg apparently had some sort of heavy unit destroyer they decided to develop one of their own. The Protoss realised that it wasn't as strong as what a protoss could come up with but faster firing.

* * *

disquiet with the birds

WE'VE BEEN having trouble with the birds. They're supposed to read the books that we give them. Fly onto people's window-ledges and just read the texts. That's the deal. But lately, there have been mutterings. Some of the birds have been saying that they disagree with our selections.

Not outright, obviously. Among themselves. Rumours. That's all that reaches us. The crows. The parrots. The woodpeckers. We'd expect it of them, frankly. But the sparrows? When the sparrows kick off, you know something's wrong. Really wrong.

They're saying that our choices are limiting. They're saying that knowledge is about more than just facts. They're saying that intelligence is more subtle. They're saying that an ability to critically evaluate one's own learning style is more the preferred thing, these days.

We have no idea what they are talking about. We only know that when we hand out Priestley's *Complete Monarchs of England*, or Volume Two of Hardwick's *Notable Dates*, they turn up their beaks and make a big show of flapping about. And they're not putting the same sort of effort into the readings as they used to. The facts will only stick in people's minds if they put some drama into it.

They won't get away with this. We've been in negotiation with some squirrels. Just because facts aren't in favour right now, doesn't mean we won't stick to the plan.

blink

EVERY TIME my father lied, he blinked. A full facial wink that was nearer to a wince, like someone had poked him with a pin. And given how my father lied just about all the time, some days he looked like an epileptic mid-fit. He'd lie about anything: the time of day, the colour of the sky, the make of his shoes. He couldn't help himself.

For instance, our very last conversation went like this:

'Dad, look. There's a wood pigeon over in the old birch tree.'

'That's not a birch tree, it's a cedar. It only looks like a birch because it's got bark-rot. You're too young to know, of course, but bark-rot was once common round here. It came across with the Lithuanian settlers. The spores were in the tiny splinters that were lodged in the soles of their famous rubber sandals.'

'Lithuanian settlers?'

'And anyway, that's not a wood-pigeon.'

His face is working ten to the dozen now.

'It's a parrot.'

* * *

Snow

IT HAS SNOWED for four days straight. We're snowed in. And because nobody can go anywhere or do anything, nothing is happening that the newspapermen can call 'news'. So they are getting twitchy, and sit at their desks playing with their calculators. They have come up with numbers about how much the snow is 'costing us'. They call this number 'lost productivity'. But yesterday, all across our little city, people lent their neighbours shovels, threw snowballs while laughing, made popcorn with their children, made love in the afternoon. What sort of numbers do we give to these things we found instead?

* * *

the new buildings

WE'VE BEEN extremely disappointed with the architects. The buildings they unveiled to us weren't at all what we were hoping for: they were squat and lumpen, and looked more like discarded breeze blocks that had been hollowed out by children. How much fun would hollowing out a breeze block be? Exactly. And when it started to rain the day after the grand opening, the red paint washed off the exterior walls, and the streets were bathed in crimson. We gave the architects our sternest looks, and asked them what they were playing at – the new buildings were meant to embody the optimism and ideals of our people as they faced the future. Their hopes. Their dreams.

The architects looked at us flatly and said, 'Well. What did you expect?' before stalking off across the building sites.

* * *

the dogs

The dogs started to speak. It was incredible to us at first. They coughed up words as though they were bits of broken stick, with a hack and a shake of the head. Like each word was painful, left splinters. We hung on their every word to begin with. The talking dogs became celebrities. 'The situation as we see it is untenable,' they might say, with a scratch of the ear, or 'the crayons are for use only in the colouring area', or 'our teeth are noisy, and this displeases us'. But gradually, we came to realise that the dogs weren't making any sense. They were, in fact, talking complete rubbish. 'The pears must be peeled before they can be eaten.' I mean, what kind of a thing to say is that? So, gradually, we cancelled their chat-show appearances, and these days they are pretty much ignored. Occasionally, you might hear in the park, 'A spiral might rightly be described as a circle ascending', but the owner will ignore it entirely. Or else snap: 'Look. Just fetch the stick, will you?'

* * *

the stone rains

WE WANTED TO SEE the stone rains for ourselves. It took us nine days to travel to the plains. They are cut off by encircling mountains, with peaks like foxes' teeth, needle-thin and close-packed. The sand on the plains is iron-red and hot. It is a mystery to us why anyone lives out there, but they do. They huddle together in a small village made almost entirely of corrugated iron.

We arrived weary and in need of food and water. Their goats came up and nuzzled us with their noses. But the villagers were less pleased to see us. We ignored their scowls and kept pointing at our mouths with bunched fingers. They grabbed at our clothes and pulled us inside. Their speech was staccato and full of odd clicks and toks, just like we had been told it would be. They talk like this so they can slip their words swiftly between the sounds of the pelting rocks.

It was then that the rains came.

Shouldn't we fetch the goats in? we asked.

No. Don't worry about the goats, the villagers replied.

At first it was just the lightest dink, and then an almost gentle dappling, like a handful of gravel tossed against a wall. But soon it grew heaver and faster, a rattling giving way to a clattering and a thundering until very soon it was just a white noise all around us, saturating everything, loosening our teeth, our skin, our thoughts. Outside the sands were being thrashed into clouds. We clutched our ears and screamed. Part terror, and part just to make a human sound in the roar. It did no good. The stone rains went on for two hours. Afterwards, we collapsed sweating and hoarse onto the floor.

When we eventually stumbled outside, we found the goats. They were dead. Not only dead, but threshed into tiny bits, practically a paste of blood and bone.

We thought you said the goats would be fine, we said.

No. We said not to worry about them, they replied.

The villagers busied themselves with the goats, and made us a parting meal. They also gave us small cups of water, which left us needing more. They said that it was always like this. We stared into the fires and didn't reply. We packed at dawn and headed back to the city. As we left, they were placing newborn babies into metal bins, and pelting the bins with stones.

It's how we prepare them for life here, they said. Now leave. You're too fat to fit into the bins, and you'd never understand anyhow.

* * *

the long way home

NOW THAT Mama's marbles are less frequently to be found where she last put them, she has become restless. We had always joked that her life was so rooted to the house and the land here, that one day the chestnut trees might claim her as one of their own. It seems we were wrong.

'I hate this place,' she said one day. 'These walls, they are the colour of Edam. This lavender – I've had my fill of its politeness. This fire, it's flames are always the same. Everything is always the same. Look at Duendo, even he is in despair. See how he sulks. Do you see his tail wagging? Do you?'

I look at Duendo. He is asleep, his tail tucked under his paw.

At first, we tried to distract her. 'Mama, guess what I got at the market today? Goat's cheese. Your favourite. Let me make you a delicious lunch.'

But Mama just said: 'Goats? Pah. I hate goats. I've had two earfuls of their bleating. It's such a whingy sound. That's all I ever see out of this window, goats snuffling and grizzling. I'd like to see ducks. Yes, ducks. Why don't you ever bring me duck's cheese? What kind of son are you anyway?'

Sometimes, we tried to reason with her: 'But Mama, you are old. Too old to start a new life. These rooms have seen your children grow. Your children's children have sat by this fire. Your children's children's children have taken their first steps in this courtyard. Isn't it a comfort to be here, cradled by these memories?'

But Mama just said: 'Memories? Pah. What good are memories to me? They are packing their bags and leaving me, one by one. I'd go too, if I could remember where I kept my suitcase. You've hidden it, haven't you, son? What a way to treat a poor old woman. And what's that quacking noise? Do you hear it?'

Mostly, though, we tried to ignore her. We'd leave her sitting by the fire, chuntering to herself, while we sat in the next room, staring at our hands and trying to keep the children out of her glare. Sometimes, if we weren't quick enough, she'd lure one to her side with the promise of biscuits, and say: 'Family? Pah. This family hate me. You should run away while you still can. Go up the track, get on to the highway, and run and run, and never look back. Do it now, before your legs become like mine, just useless brittle sticks.'

And then she'd slump into a sulk, and some of the children would cry, and we'd bicker among ourselves until Mama shooed us all out of the door, using her words like a broom. She'd bash at my ankles with them, saying 'I know what you're thinking. You want to take me out behind the garage and drop me in the quicksand, don't you? Plop! Then I'd be no more trouble to you. Don't deny it. I see it in your eyes', and then she'd slam the door in my face and leave me standing on the step.

And then, one day, after a particularly testing visit, which had required us to fetch several of the children back off the highway, I drove back to her house and said: 'Mama, it's time. We've found a new place for you. Grab what you can.'

In two minutes, she's sitting next to me in the car. Toothbrush in one hand, Duendo under the other arm.

'Is it far?' she asks.

'You've no idea how far,' I reply.

Then I drive to the end of the track and onto the highway. We talk of new beginnings, old habits, fresh pastures, clean starts. And when I get to the big roundabout by the garage, I go round.

Seven times.

Then I drive back down the highway, along the track, and pull up outside Mama's house again, and say: 'Here you are, Mama. Your new home.'

She hops from the car and runs into the house. Her eyes alive, her legs steady.

'Oh, my,' she says, inhaling deeply. 'Just smell. Lavender. My favourite. It's such a sensual smell, don't you think?'

'Yes, Mama.'

'And look!' She rushes to the window. 'Goats! How I love goats! Their bleats are like birdsong to my soul. Such happy creatures, don't you think?'

'Yes, Mama.'

'These walls – so bright and cheerful. And the fire, so alive with mischief. And look – even Duendo is contented.'

We look down at Duendo, who is curled up under the table, his tail under his paw.

'It's perfect,' she says. 'Just the change I needed. I'll be happy here, my son.'

'Yes, Mama.'

'But get that duck out of here, will you? It's looking at me funny.'

'Yes, Mama,' I say.

* * *

cleaning the river

THE RIVERBED needed a jolly good clean. But there was nowhere to store the water in the meantime. So we gave everybody a quota of water which they would be required to store while the cleaning took place. The quota was 200 litres per person. The deliveries went smoothly, for the most part – a fleet of trucks moved swiftly through the streets, dispensing the river through a specially adapted hose. Some people had prepared containers specially, or else uncovered disused garden ponds. Many people gamely poured their quota into their baths. Others took a more ad hoc approach, and filled whatever came to hand when the delivery turned up: pots and pans, recycled bottles and jars. Some people wanted to know which bit of the river they were looking after exactly, and we had to explain that rivers didn't really work like that.

All in all, nobody seemed to mind too much, and we remember it as a time of considerable public-spiritedness.

The cleaning was a greatsuccess. We were soon able to go round and collect the water again, and pour it back into the river, which now ran as freely as could be. It is true that it is some centimetres shallower than once it was. We think some people have grown used to having 'their' bit of the river at home, and have been reluctant to give it back. We don't make a fuss about it. It will all sort itself out in time. Already, when we stand quietly on the bridges at night, we can hear the soft trickles and splashes as people pour back a jarful or two, trying hard not to be noticed. We look the other way. What with the river being now so fast and fresh and clear that it seems churlish to make a fuss.

1997: Faraj Sarkoohi

Written for 'Because writers speak their minds', the fiftieth anniversary campaign of International PEN's Writers in Prison Committee.

We do not like
the words you choose.
So, we have chosen
some for you:
I flew to Germany.
I stayed for a month.
I contacted no one.
You are mistaken.
Everything is normal.
I am fine. I am fine.
Isn't that how you tell a story?
Now. Come with us.

the unfrozen

AT FIRST, the cryonic freezing was a terrific success. Everyone got pretty excited about popping themselves in a refrigerator when their bodies were done in, and being thawed out later on when medical science had got a bit smarter. Funerals suddenly became much more positive affairs: no more slipping between two velvet curtains into the wheezing lungs of a furnace. No. For those left behind, it was more like waving someone off on a cruise which you were joining later at another port. A bit sad, but you knew they'd be comfortably numbed and you'd see them soon enough at Antibes. From now on, it was only ever to be adieu. And soon enough, everyone's prayers were answered. A few big strides in medicine and we were ready to start thawing people out.

Which was when everything started to go a bit wrong.

It turned out that while their loved ones had been in the deep freeze, most of the living had got on with the business of living. It turned out that the living had got used to being on their own; had moved abroad; had remarried. It turned out that the living weren't all that keen on their loved ones coming back to life after all. It turned out that, frankly, having your frozen husband or wife turn up was more than a little annoying.

We lived with this awkward situation for a while – the frozen getting together in bars and clubs to drink and moan about how they felt displaced, forgotten, unloved. Or else, if loved, then loved in a sort of distant way, like you might love a decrepit and slightly greasy family cat. You wish it well, but you wouldn't want to cuddle it or have it in your bed or anything. It's like we're seeing life through a fine layer of cling film, they'd say.

What are you talking about? Are you still here? We'd snap back.

And then, one day, all 276 of the unfrozen vanished. Just plain disappeared. We don't know where they went. It was completely baffling to us. But we were also secretly a little relieved. We looked for them for a bit, but after that it seemed for the best that we leave them be. It's what they would have wanted.

* * *

lightning

THE FIRST TIME was as unexpected as your leaving. It was the wonky wiring on the car's cigarette lighter. Mid-jolt, I remembered the feel of your touch, your fingers gently on my spine. I sat there in a daze, the faint smell of burnt hair in the air, my mind six months away.

The second time, it was changing the lightbulb in the old lamp. The shock was like a slap from all directions at once. And while it still smarted, I could see you again like I haven't since that night. Your silhouette as you moved in front of the window.

Last night I deliberately stuck a fork in the toaster, and in between the jolt that's like being plunged into an iced swimming pool, and the point where I fell back and whacked my head on the worktop, I saw your face again. As it was when I watched you read, when you laughed in the café that time, when we kissed by the old barges.

Tonight I'm going to grab the frayed wiring on the iron. With both wet hands.

And then tomorrow, my love? I'm going to work out how to get struck by lightning.

* * *

the museum of the sea

IN THE EARLY DAYS we focused mostly on clarifying what the Museum of the Sea was to be. Which is to say, we mainly followed Mallard around with our notebooks, while he extemporised on his vision. He spent a lot of time in his rowing boat, out in the bay. We followed in boats of our own. Making notes while rowing at the same time was quite tricky, we recall. It was also difficult to hear – the sound of waves lapping is surprisingly loud. Mallard seemed oblivious and went on talking away, and waving his arms all over the place. We tried to draw conclusions from his gestures. Charles wrote down: 'jellyfish', 'harpoon' and 'oscillating water column'. Mallard would frequently lean over the side of the boat and dip his hands into the water, bringing up palmfuls of brine, proffering these as though by way of explanation. We would nod and make it look like we understood perfectly well what he was on about, while trying not to let the laptops get too wet, or let the oars accidentally slip into the water. Later, when we were back on shore, I asked Charles how he had known what to write. He said he was just 'riding the wave', whatever that means.

THE COASTAL hike was also rather fraught, if we're honest. For some reason Mallard chose an exceptionally windy day to head out. The coastline that is closest to us is treacherous to say the least. Loose shingle followed by crumbling chalk followed by stretches of path strewn with boulders and boot-snagging heather. Mallard marched on ahead, his umbrella raised in the air. We followed, the winds that whipped around the headland snatching the air from our lungs as we stumbled along. Occasionally he would stop and gesture expansively out to sea. We would write a few desultory notes and then plunge onwards.

When we arrived at the cove, Mallard picked his way deftly down to the shore, his sights fixed on the cave that was half obscured by fallen rocks. We caught up with him just as he was concluding what must have been some kind of rousing oratory. His words echoed back at us from the mouth of the cave: 'None none of of this this is is the the sort sort of of thing thing that that will will appear appear in in the the Museum Museum of of the the Sea Sea.'

THE DAY at the Aqua-Park was really quite eventful. We set up the video cameras and got some excellent footage of the penguins, and the fast shutter speeds really came into their own when capturing the seals mid-backflip. Mallard paced up and down behind us shouting encouragement. We all had a go holding out the bait, and the close-ups of the killer whale leaping up and brushing against our fingertips were spectacular. It was a struggle for some of us to get the wetsuits on, but it was worth it to swim with the dolphin. The keepers also said that it was the first time they had ever seen twenty-five people all swim with one dolphin, and it's true that the little fellow did have to thrash up a fair old amount of foam just to get moving. Afterwards, as we sat on the side of the pool, catching our breath and bandaging Peter's arm, the keepers said that it was highly unusual for a dolphin to turn like that, what with them being so highly evolved and all. But we could tell that they were laying the blame pretty squarely at our feet. We stared at our flippers and didn't say much until Mallard brought the mini-bus round. Back at the studio we stuck the photographs up on the walls and pointed out the ones we thought captured the events of the day best. Mallard seemed quite drawn to the picture which caught Peter's unfortunate run-in with Slippy. He remarked on how he had never imagined dolphins to have so many teeth. Then he said: 'Of course, none of *this* is suitable for the Museum of the Sea.'

AS SOON as we arrived on the beach, Mallard unloaded twenty-five sets of buckets and spades off the back of his beach buggy, and set us to work on building sandcastles. He also said that we should remove our shoes and jackets, and advised that our silk ties might suffer a little if they came in contact with the salt water. We appreciated the warnings. As we beavered away, shaping and perfecting our castles, sculpting ramparts and turrets, and digging moats for the tides to fill, Mallard clambered up onto the lifeguard's tall chair, and watched.

By the end of the day, the array of sandcastles was truly impressive. Some were enormous high towers encrusted with shells and dried starfish and stood taller than a man. Some were precarious constructions of pillars and platforms, which seemed to defy the natural properties of sand. Some were long and wide, with intricate patterns of pebbles running along the outside, and moats that ran for several metres in all directions. All day we ran back and forth through the soft water-logged sand, fetching shells and seaweed and pebbles, leaving those little sucking footprints behind us. We have to say that we surpassed ourselves. Charles was so taken with his own creation that he tried to scoop some parts of it up and put it in his briefcase, but grains of sand got lodged in the clasp and made an unpleasant crunch when he tried to close it. Mallard strode among the castles nodding seriously to himself. As the sun began to set he sent us all off to buy ourselves ice cream, but alas we had left it too late, and although we found a waste bin over-flowing with Cornetto wrappers, we realised that the van must have already gone home. We returned a little downcast. The castles had vanished. One glance at Mallard and we knew the truth. All that was left of our day's handiwork were little sandy mounds, with Mallard's flip flop prints all over them. 'I hardly need to say, gentlemen, that none of this is at all fit for the Museum of the Sea,' he said flatly, and stalked off to the car park.

MALLARD HIRED a beach hut and called a meeting. We had dried our notebooks on the radiators in the studio, and were ready and waiting. He wished to clarify, he said, a few further things about what the Museum of the Sea was not. He looked at each of us in turn: the Museum of the Sea is not an aquarium; the Museum of the Sea is not a theme park; the Museum of the Sea is not a repository for artefacts pertaining to exploration, sailing, shipping, or maritime endeavours; the Museum of the Sea is not an educational facility aimed at addressing environmental 'concerns' in an 'accessible' way; the Museum of the Sea is not a curiosity shop for the display of aquatic artefacts, nor a storehouse of a taxonomy on the seas, such as comically ugly fish which have been rendered thus by the crushing pressures of the ocean deeps; the Museum of the Sea will not mention in any way the crushing pressures of the ocean deeps; the Museum of the Sea will not be a place for re-enactments of early attempts to cross the oceans, by means of canoe, raft or otherwise; the Museum of the Sea will not countenance the display of ocean-related painting, sculpture, tapestry, poetry, myth, song or dance. The Museum of the Sea will not contain any signage written in easily digestible factoids; the Museum of the Sea will not, in fact, contain any signage at all; the Museum of the Sea will have no interactive display units; in the Museum of the Sea, there will be no audio guides. I'm sure it goes without saying that the Museum of the Sea will certainly not have a shop. There will be no pencils with Museum of the

Sea written down the side in gold lettering; there will be no Museum of the Sea erasers or pencil cases.

We all sat in silence for the longest time. Eventually, Peter raised his good arm and asked the question that we were all thinking. But Mallard raised a hand and silenced him: 'Let me say only this,' he said. 'When I go to an aquarium I do not marvel at the fish. I do not marvel at the crustaceans. I do not marvel at the anemones. When I walk through the glass tunnels, I do not marvel at the sharks overhead. I marvel at the water, the beautiful tanks of water. I see the wood, not the trees.'

We were chastened by these words. Although out of the corner of my eye, I noticed that Charles had jotted down in his notebook: 'Trees made of water?'

ONE NIGHT in the bar, Mallard gathered us all around his table. He asked us to put down our drinks, close our eyes and make ourselves comfortable. He said:

'Imagine that you are floating in the ocean, right out in the middle, where all you can see in any direction is just ocean and more ocean. Now, take a deep breath, and hold it. You begin to sink. First of all, you sink down through the warm water to a depth of two hundred metres. When you look up, you can still see the glow of the surface above you. You have sunk through the photic layer. You keep on sinking down. The water is colder. The light is almost gone. You're at one thousand metres now. There is no light at all at this depth. You sink further. The temperature is just a few degrees above zero. You might see a giant squid at this depth, or perhaps a Black Swallower. Except you won't really be able to see anything at all, because it is pitch black, a total freezing blackness the likes of which it is not possible to experience anywhere else in the universe. A blackness that is crushing you to the tune of nearly five long tons of force per square inch. You are now nearly six kilometres from the surface, and still sinking. Think just how far six kilometres really is. But you haven't come to rest yet, you keep sinking, past even the bed of the deepest oceans on earth, into the hadal zone. The dead zone. This is the water in the deepest trenches at the bottom of the deepest oceans in the world. If you could see, you might glimpse a blind tube worm leeching an existence on the side of a black smoker. The tube worms live on sulphur. Their bodies are transparent. If any of these creatures were to float upwards, the lack of extreme pressure would kill them. Imagine what it must be like, to need that crushing pressure on you at all times, just to stay alive.

'You may open your eyes now.'

We opened our eyes, gasping for breath. Several people had passed out, and others dashed for the door to take in fresh air or be sick. Mallard seemed rather pleased with himself. 'Anyway,' he said, 'we won't be making reference to any of that in the Museum of the Sea either.'

BY NOW, we had many volumes filled with our notes concerning items which would not appear in the Museum of the Sea. I had spent several weeks painstakingly colouring a map clearly showing the designations of all the oceans and the seas: the Atlantic; the Pacific; the Indian; the Southern; the Arctic; the Caspian; the Dead; many others. Next to each ocean, Mallard had written, 'Don't mention this in the Museum of the Sea', and appended a little arrow, pointing from the words to the names of the various oceans. Then there were the meticulous diagrams detailing all tidal movements across an entire lunar month. I had copied each diagram out by hand, and Mallard had added to it, in neat pencil, writing in the top left-hand corner: 'This will not be appearing in the Museum of the Sea.' The scientific papers were also piled high, each one printed out on the special paper which Mallard had ordered. Pick up a copy of, for instance, 'Rupture of the Cell Envelope by Decompression of the Deep-Sea Methanogen by C B Park and D S Clark (2002)' and hold it up to the light and you'll see the watermark: 'This information must not be included in the Museum of the Sea.' The same goes for print-outs of the complete transcripts of every single shipping forecast. Our store rooms are filled with coral, shells, fossils of ancient sea creatures; maps from almost every century, showing the locations of trade routes, or treasure, or sea-monsters; we have a complete set of all the uniforms of all the naval forces around the globe. Each artefact bears a tiny laser-printed tag, saying: 'Not for inclusion in the Museum of the Sea.'

THAT LAST DAY, Mallard convened us all on the old oil rig. It had been derelict for some time, and in truth we all admired its shabby grandeur, the casual atmosphere of menace. As we slipped past the DO NOT ENTER signs and over the barriers with DANGER written on them in orange lettering, we could see Mallard already standing on the main viewing platform. As usual, we had to gather close to hear Mallard's words, before the salt air snatched them from his mouth and flung them out to sea. He said:

'I have a story to tell you. There was once an island in the Pacific Ocean. It was a small island, no more than a mile across. It was blessed with golden beaches and rich soils and a rotation of rain and sunshine which presented the islanders with an embarrassment of bounty. All who lived there were content, and the island's chief saw to it that this happy state of affairs was given every chance to prosper. He made sure that the islanders were generous towards one another and when he was, infrequently, called upon to adjudicate in a dispute, he was regarded as just and fair. The islanders had no knowledge of life outside of their island, and in every direction their horizon showed unceasing, unbroken ocean. They passed their days fishing, dancing, tending their crops, raising their children, and racing each other to see who could swim around the island the fastest.

'And then, one day, after a terrible storm had raged for three days and three nights, the islanders noticed that there was a ship floating in their shallows. Its sails were in tatters, its masts were broken, it was listing heavily. The islanders were curious and rowed out to the stricken vessel. On board they found just a dozen survivors. The islanders helped the survivors onto their canoes and took them back to their island, where they fed them and tended to their injuries. Soon the sailors were much recovered, and wished to thank their rescuers, but the islanders had such a bountiful life that there was nothing that they wished for. The sailors felt that offering the ship's three remaining barrels of salt-beef was a poor exchange for their lives, and just about everything else had been lost in the storm. But they did have one thing: among the cargo on the ship was a meteorological balloon. It was a small balloon with a seat slung beneath it, in the French style. Also in the hold was the sack of iron filings and the vessels of hydrochloric acid needed to create the hydrogen gas needed to get the balloon airborne.

'Through much arm-waving and smiling, the captain managed to communicate that the men and women of the tribe, should they so wish, could sit in the balloon and, by means of a gas that was lighter than air, rise far above the island, up to where the gulls flew. The islanders were excited, and milled around expectantly as the sailors set about mixing the gas. The chief of the island made it known that he wished to be the first to ride in the balloon.

'Once the balloon was fully inflated, the sailors secured it to a large tree, and the chief of the island, grinning from ear to ear, took his place in the seat. It was an extraordinary sight, their chief, in full ceremonial head-dress, sitting under a bobbing balloon in the manner of sitting on a child's swing. And then, slowly, the sailors began to slacken the rope which allowed the balloon to rise. For nearly a minute the balloon floated up, hardly deviating left or right on that sunny and windless day. All seemed to be going well. The chief waved down from the balloon. He seemed relaxed.

'And then, suddenly, as the balloon reached the limit of the rope, the chief started screaming. Even two hundred feet in the air, his screams could be heard clearly by all those below. They hauled on the rope and brought the balloon back to earth. Had the chief had a fit of vertigo? Was he perhaps afraid of falling? Had he decided that the balloon was some terrible piece of black magic? As soon as his feet touched the ground, he fled into the forest. The islanders and the sailors stood frozen, watching each other, as the chief's screams slowly faded into the distance.

'Perhaps everything would have been all right if the sailors hadn't panicked. They dashed into the shallows and tried to clamber into one of the islander's canoes. The islanders, fearing that their chief's screams signalled something truly unspeakable, fell on the sailors and killed them with spears. Then, revulsed by their own actions, they too fled into the forest, leaving the bodies to be washed back onto the beach by the tide, streaking the sand with blood.'

We held our breath. Mallard was beckoning us towards him. 'It is said,' he almost whispered, 'by others who visited the island later and found its lands untilled, its people dishevelled and drunken, and its shorelines littered with debris, that what happened to the chief up there that day was this: he saw with his own eyes the insignificance of his island in the vast ocean. He saw the ocean stretching off for ever in all directions. He saw that his own island, all the people he knew, his entire world, was just a yellow speck, a precarious blip, a mere nothing. It is said that the realisation drove him mad. The whole island fell under a terrible pall from which it never recovered.'

Mallard stared at us with a look of soft-boiled resignation

in his eyes. The sea rolled behind him. The wind ripped at the pages of our notebooks, which flapped in our hands like angry seagulls.

'The question is,' said Mallard. 'Does such a story belong in the Museum of the Sea?'

Some say it was Peter who snapped first. Others say it was Charles. I have to admit that even though we all rushed at Mallard as one, I felt that it was my hands which were round his throat first. And, yes, we know that such an act is indefensible, but all we can say is that as we heaved Mallard over the railings and watched him plunge down into the sea, several of us would swear that we saw a smile on his lips. And as he surfaced for a second time between the waves, was he trying to say something to us? Did he perhaps shout, before he went under that final time, 'Put this into the Museum of the Sea'? We rather think he did.

* * *

Printed in Great Britain
by Amazon